W9-CCC-488

Three Little Kittens

For Jamie, Jacob, Nathaniel, and Mariska

Clarion Books
a Houghton Mifflin Company imprint
215 Park Avenue South, New York, NY 10003
Copyright © 1986 by Paul Galdone
For information about permission to reproduce
selections from this book, write to Permissions,
Houghton Mifflin Company, 215 Park Avenue South, New York, NY 10003.
Printed in the USA
BVG 30 29 28 27 26 25 24 23 22 21
Library of Congress Cataloging-in-Publication Data. Galdone, Paul. Three little kittens.
Summary: Three little kittens lose, find, soil, and wash their mittens. 1. Nursery rhymes.
2. Children's poetry.
[1. Cats—Poetry.   2. Nursery rhymes]   I. Title.   PZ8.3.G1218Th   1986
398'.8   86-2655   ISBN 0-89919-426-5   PA ISBN 0-89919-796-5

Three Little Kittens

Illustrated by
PAUL GALDONE

CLARION BOOKS
NEW YORK

Three

Little Kittens

they lost their
mittens,
and they began
to cry,

"Oh, Mother Dear, we sadly fear
Our mittens we have lost!"

CATNIP

chopped   minced

blended   ground

seed   roots

leaves

FLOUR

"What! lost your mittens,
you naughty kittens!

9

Then you shall have no pie."

The
three little kittens

12

found their mittens
and they began to cry,

13

"Oh! Mother Dear, see here, see here.

Our mittens we have found."

"What!
found your mittens,
you good little kittens,

purrrrr... purrrr... purr

Then
you shall
have
some pie."
"Purr,
purr,
purr."

17

The three little kittens

put on their mittens
and soon ate up the pie.

"Oh! Mother Dear, we greatly fear
Our mittens we have soiled."

"What! soiled your mittens,
you naughty kittens!"

Then they
began to sigh,
"Meow,
meow,
meow!"

23

The three little kittens

washed their mittens,

and hung them up to dry.

"Oh! Mother Dear,
look here, look here,

Our mittens
we have
washed."

29

"What! washed your mittens,
you darling kittens!

But
hush!
I smell
a rat
close
by."

31

"Yes, we smell a rat close by.
Meow, meow, *meow!*"